The New Adventures of
MARY-KATE & ASHLEY ™

The Case Of
Camp Pom-Pom

Look for more great books in
~The New Adventures of~
MARY-KATE & ASHLEY™
series:

The Case Of The Great Elephant Escape
The Case Of The Summer Camp Caper
The Case Of The Surfing Secret
The Case Of The Green Ghost
The Case Of The Big Scare Mountain Mystery
The Case Of The Slam Dunk Mystery
The Case Of The Rock Star's Secret
The Case Of The Cheerleading Camp Mystery
The Case Of The Flying Phantom
The Case Of The Creepy Castle
The Case Of The Golden Slipper
The Case Of The Flapper 'Napper
The Case Of The High Seas Secret
The Case Of The Logical I Ranch
The Case Of The Dog Camp Mystery
The Case Of The Screaming Scarecrow
The Case Of The Jingle Bell Jinx
The Case Of The Game Show Mystery
The Case Of The Mall Mystery
The Case Of The Weird Science Mystery
The Case Of Camp Crooked Lake
The Case Of The Giggling Ghost
The Case Of The Candy Cane Clue
The Case Of The Hollywood Who-Done-It
The Case Of The Sundae Surprise
The Case Of Clue's Circus Caper

and coming soon

The Case Of The Tattooed Cat

The New Adventures of
MARY-KATE & ASHLEY ™

The Case Of
Camp Pom-Pom

by Heather Alexander

HarperEntertainment
An Imprint of HarperCollins*Publishers*

A PARACHUTE PRESS BOOK

PARACHUTE PRESS

Parachute Publishing, L.L.C.
156 Fifth Avenue
New York, NY 10010

DUALSTAR PUBLICATIONS

Dualstar Publications
c/o Thorne and Company
A Professional Law Corporation
1801 Century Park East
Los Angeles, CA 90067

☰HarperEntertainment

An Imprint of HarperCollins*Publishers*
10 East 53rd Street, New York, NY 10022

Cheers on pages 5 and 35 written by Erin Sullivan

ISBN 0-06-009337-4

HarperCollins®, ☰®, and HarperEntertainment™ are trademarks of
HarperCollins Publishers Inc.

First printing: July 2003

Printed in the United States of America

mary-kateandashley.com
America Online Keyword: mary-kateandashley

10 9 8 7 6 5 4 3 2 1

1

WHERE IS KRIS?

"Eagles! Eagles! We fly high!
Eagles! Eagles! Touch the sky!
Shout it out! We are the best!
Eagles fly above the rest!"

All the girls in our cheerleading squad jumped up in the air and touched their toes at the same time.

One of our camp counselors, Fiona, blew her whistle. "Good job, girls!" she

said. "Let's all take a five-minute break."

Her blond braids bounced as she jogged over to me. "Mary-Kate, you're up next. Are you ready?"

"I sure am!" I gave Fiona a big smile.

We were so lucky to have Fiona as our squad leader. During the school year, she's a cheerleader here at Orange Grove College, where our camp takes place. She's so peppy it's hard not to be peppy too. But right now my stomach felt as if it were doing handsprings.

I turned to my sister, Ashley. "Tell me again why *I* have to be the one to climb to the top of the pyramid?"

Ashley fixed her strawberry-blond ponytail. "Because you are the best flyer, Mary-Kate," she said.

Our squad at Camp Pom-Pom is called the Eagles. That's why we're going to do a really high-flying stunt at the *Cheer Off!*

competition. We are going to build a pyramid.

First, I climb to the top. Then our squad mascot, Pom the Wonder Bird, runs onto the field and does a double back handspring. After that Pom drags over a cushion shaped like a bird's nest. Then I'm supposed to jump off the top of the pyramid into the nest.

There's only one problem—I'm afraid of heights.

"Uh-oh. Here come the Hornets," Ashley said.

A group of girls in yellow-and-black cheering uniforms ran toward us. Our squad and the Hornets are in the finals for the camp's *Cheer Off!* competition.

Last week, we beat the four other squads—the Tigers, Bears, Sharks, and Dragons—for a spot in the finals. It's just two days away!

"Eagles, Eagles, what's the news? Your big silly bird is gonna lose!"

The Hornets whooped and hollered. Then their bumblebee mascot did the most amazing backflip!

For a moment all our squad could do was stare. That is, everyone stared except Patty O'Leary. Her brown ponytail bounced as she screamed, "The Eagles are *not* going to lose! We're going to crush you like the insects you are!"

Patty lives next door to me and Ashley at home. Sometimes we call her Princess Patty because she is so spoiled. And she hates to lose!

"We float like butterflies," chanted the Hornets, *"and we sting like bees!"*

Then the Hornets did running cartwheels back to their side of the practice field.

"Whoa! Tory is really good," Kris McKenzie said.

Tory Orsini plays the Hornets' bumble-bee mascot.

"You're better than she is!" Briana Williams told Kris. "Pom rules!"

Kris is our mascot. She plays Pom the Wonder Bird. During mascot tryouts she made everyone fall down laughing. Her long arms and legs work perfectly with the Pom costume.

"I *know* we are going to beat the Hornets," Brooke Barton said. "We have been so in the groove this week."

Brooke is ten years old—just like me and Ashley—and she's our squad captain. She always wears purple and yellow hair ribbons for luck. Purple and yellow are our squad colors.

"We're so great, we're so fine, we'll beat the Hornets anytime!" cried Caitlin Sullivan, another girl on our squad.

"There she goes again!" I said to Ashley.

We giggled. Caitlin is our cheer writer. She says almost everything in cheer!

"Let's get to work on the pyramid," Fiona said. "Kris, hurry and put your costume on."

Kris ran off to get the Pom costume. The rest of our squad started to build the pyramid.

First Briana, Caitlin, Patty, and Brooke formed the base—the very bottom of the pyramid. Then Fiona and two other counselors helped Ashley and Emma Layton stand on the other girls' shoulders. When everyone was in place, the counselors helped me climb up.

I wobbled as I placed my feet on Ashley's and Emma's shoulders. *Please don't fall, please don't fall*, I chanted to myself.

Emma's shoulders shook as I slowly straightened up. Her necklace with the silver megaphone charm swayed back and forth until she steadied herself.

Breathe, breathe, I said to myself....

Okay, I'm up. I'm dizzy, but I'm up. I let out a breath. Now it was time for me to jump into the cushion.

I *slowly* looked down—but Kris wasn't there!

"Where's Kris?" I squeaked.

I looked *slowly* to the left. No Kris. I looked *slowly* to the right—and there she was, running toward us.

But she wasn't wearing the Pom costume. And she didn't have the cushion! How was I going to get down?

"Pom is gone!" she yelled. "Someone stole our mascot costume!"

THE MISSING MASCOT

W*hoa!* Everyone turned to look at Kris, and their weight under me shifted.

"Help!" I cried as I lost my balance. "I'm falling!"

Fiona and the other counselors caught me. They placed me gently on the grass.

"Are you okay, Mary-Kate?" Ashley asked.

I took a deep, shaky breath. "I'm fine."

Fiona turned to Kris. "What happened?"

"I went back to my room to get the Pom

costume," Kris said. She was panting from running so fast. "I left it on my bed right before lunch. But it wasn't there!"

"Did you look everywhere?" I asked.

"Yes!" Kris said. "It's gone!"

Ashley turned to Patty, who is Kris's dorm mate. "Did you put the costume anywhere?"

Patty wrinkled her nose. "No way! I try not to touch that big bird. Its feathers are always shedding on my sweaters."

"Who took it then?" Emma asked. Her freckled face looked worried.

Before we could ask any more questions, we heard the Hornets heading our way again.

"Listen, guys," Fiona said. "Let's keep quiet about the missing mascot costume. We don't want to lose *Cheer Off!* because we don't have a mascot."

We all nodded.

The Hornets chanted, *"We've got it! You want it! You lost it! You need it!"*

Patty stomped her foot and threw her pom-poms to the ground. "I knew it! You stole our mascot!" she cried.

I groaned. Leave it to Patty to open her big mouth after we all agreed not to say anything!

"Take your mascot? Get real!" Tory said.

"Then what are you cheering about?" Patty narrowed her eyes at Tory.

The Hornets started their chant again:

"We've got it! You want it!
You lost it! You need it!
SPIRIT! SPIRIT!"

Then they turned and ran off across the field.

"Oh, *spirit*." Patty shook her head in disbelief. "That's not what they are cheering about. They don't want us to win *Cheer Off!* I'm sure they took Pom."

"Well," Ashley said. "Before we can accuse the Hornets, we should search really hard for the costume." She turned to Kris. "It was in your room the last time you saw it, right?"

Ashley is very logical. She likes to think first, then act.

Kris nodded.

"Let's go!" I took off running. I like to act, then think.

We ran to our dorm.

The dorms at Orange Grove College look like white farmhouses. There are six dorms lined up around a grassy green square. Each squad at the camp has its own dorm.

We paired up and looked all over our dorm. Ashley and I were in the kitchen when we heard Emma and Briana yelling from the basement, "Everyone! Come quick!"

We rushed downstairs to the basement, where the laundry room is. Emma and

Briana pointed to a large laundry cart. Inside the cart, under a pile of dirty clothes, was Pom the Wonder Bird!

Kris held up the costume. "How did it get in there?"

Pom the Wonder Bird looked like a giant parrot. It was covered in yellow and white feathers and wore a white sweatshirt with #1 painted in purple on the front of the shirt.

"I bet the Hornets did this," Patty said. "I bet they hid Pom to make trouble!"

"We'll figure it out later," Fiona said. She looked at her watch. "Let's hustle back to the practice field, girls. We're late for camp photos!"

We hurried to the field. All the other squads were already there. We lined up between the Hornets and the Bears. Mr. Willard, the photographer, snapped a group picture of the entire camp.

Then Mr. Willard came over to our

squad. "Hello, Eagles!" he shouted. "Ready for your close-up?"

It was our turn to get our squad picture taken.

"Kris, put on the costume—quick!" Fiona said. "It's a good thing we found it. We need our mascot."

Brooke shook her head, and a purple ribbon flew off. "I wish we never found the costume," she said, picking up the ribbon. "Cheerleading is about *cheers*, not silly mascots!"

"Mascots are important too," Emma said. "They make the crowd laugh and add a lot of spirit."

Emma had tried out to play Pom, too, but everyone had thought Kris was funnier.

"I have a great idea," said Brooke. "Let's get into our pyramid for the picture!"

I gulped. I didn't think I could climb all the way up there again.

"Um…I think we should just pose with our pom-poms," I said. "It'll be faster that way. It's almost time for dinner."

The dinner bell was ringing, so no one argued. *Yes! Saved by the bell!*

We all posed with our pom-poms high in the air, and Mr. Willard snapped the picture.

"Wake up! Wake up! It's time to wake!
Time to boogie, time to shake!
Eagles! Eagles! Don't be late!
Get up! Get up! It's almost eight!"

Caitlin chanted up and down the halls, banging on our doors. I sat up in bed and turned off my alarm clock. "Who needs an alarm clock with Caitlin around?" I said.

Ashley yawned. "Come on, Mary-Kate. Let's beat Patty to the shower. You know how she likes to hog it."

We gathered our plastic buckets with

our toothbrushes, toothpaste, soap, and shampoo and started down the hall to the bathroom.

"Good morning, guys." Fiona jogged up to us. From her sweaty shirt and shorts, I could tell she'd already been out for a run.

"Big thunderstorm last night," she said. "The field's completely soaked. Puddles everywhere. We'll practice in the gym today, okay?"

"Okay," Ashley said. "See you there."

We took fast showers and hurried back to our room. I braided my wet hair and threw on a pair of purple shorts and a white tank top. Ashley pulled on white shorts, a yellow shirt, and a white sweat-shirt. She began to comb out her hair.

I sighed. I'm always ready *way* before Ashley. I looked around the room for something to do while I waited for her. And then I got a great idea!

I went to my dresser and pulled the bottom drawer all the way out. Next I pulled the middle drawer out halfway. Then I climbed to the top of the dresser, using the drawers as stairs.

I crouched on top of the dresser for a second, then straightened up slowly until I was standing.

"Mary-Kate! What are you doing? Did you see a mouse or something?" Ashley leaped onto her bed.

"No. Get down, Ashley. I'm just practicing," I said.

"Practicing what?" Ashley asked.

"Being at the top of the pyramid," I said. "I have only one day left to get used to being up so high. The *Cheer Off!* competition is tomorrow."

I took a deep breath and tried not to look down. I knew looking down would make me dizzy.

"Oh. Good idea, Mary-Kate." Ashley opened and closed her dresser drawer. "Did you take my hair dryer?"

"No. Why?" I felt as if I was about to pitch forward. I closed my eyes tightly. *Hold it, hold it,* I told myself. *Steady.*

"It's missing," Ashley said.

"I'm sure it's around somewhere. You can use mine for now," I said.

"Yours is no good," Ashley said. "Mine is that super-high-powered dryer Mom got for me at the hair salon."

I opened my eyes and glanced out the window.

Brooke and Kris were running across the meadow toward the dorm, waving their arms and screaming. I couldn't hear what they were saying.

"Ashley!" I said. "Help me down, quick! Something's wrong!"

3

ON THE CASE

Ashley and I ran downstairs. Brooke and Kris burst through the front door.

"Pom is gone again!" Brooke yelled.

"What?" Fiona asked. "Are you sure?"

"Totally sure," Kris said. "After practice last night I put Pom away in our equipment shed. But when Brooke and I went to get our stuff for practice this morning, Pom wasn't there!"

Patty clenched her fists. "It's those

Hornets again! I know it! They stole Pom!"

"We need to find the costume!" Kris wailed. "I haven't practiced the pyramid stunt with the costume on yet."

"Let's pair up and look for it," Fiona said.

We searched our dorm from the top floor to the basement, but this time we couldn't find Pom the Wonder Bird anywhere. The time, it was really gone!

Our squad trudged to the dining hall for breakfast. No one said anything. Then we went to the gym and huddled together on the bleachers. The other campers' voices and feet echoed off the gym's walls.

"Are we going to be allowed to compete in *Cheer Off!* without a mascot?" Patty asked Fiona.

"I don't know," Fiona said.

I had never seen her look so un-peppy before.

Emma twirled her curly brown hair

around her fingers. "I'm sure we'll find Pom if we keep looking," she said.

Brooke sat up straight. Her face lit up. "I think we should change our routine. You know, put in more cheers and stunts—just in case we don't find Pom in time."

Patty pointed across the gym to the Hornets. "Well, I think we should go over there and tell the Hornets to give Pom back!"

"No way, no way, are they gonna say, that they took our mascot, hey, hey, hey!" Caitlin chanted.

"Any way she rhymes it," I said, "Caitlin's right about that."

"Then what are we going to do?" Kris said.

I looked at Ashley. I could tell she was thinking the same thing I was thinking.

"Ashley and I are pretty good at solving mysteries," I said.

Ashley and I are detectives. We run the

Olsen and Olsen Detective Agency out of the attic of our house. And we have solved tons of mysteries.

Ashley grinned. "As of right now, the Trenchcoat Twins are on the case!"

Our squad jumped up and cheered. Caitlin made up a chant:

"The costume vanishes without a trace.
But have no fear!
Give a cheer!
The Trenchcoat Twins are on the case!"

I gave Caitlin a thumbs-up. It's fun to have your own personal cheerleader!

"The first thing we need to do is get our detective backpack from our room," Ashley said. "Fiona, is it okay if we start investigating right now?"

"We'll start warming up without you," said Fiona. "But hurry back!"

She gave me a silver key. "Here's the key to the equipment shed in case you need it."

Ashley and I raced out of the gym. Our sneakers squished through the wet grass as we hurried to our dorm. Up in our room, Ashley grabbed our detective backpack. It was filled with all kinds of detective supplies.

Our Great-grandma Olive is a famous detective. She taught us everything we know about solving mysteries. And one of the most important things she taught us was always to be prepared.

"First we should check out the shed for clues," Ashley said. "That's where Kris put the costume last night."

"Good idea," I said. "Let's go!"

All the equipment sheds were behind the gym. Each squad uses a different shed. We headed toward the Eagles' shed.

On the way, Ashley pulled out her detec-

tive notebook and a pencil. "Who has a motive for stealing Pom?" she asked.

A motive is the reason someone does something.

"The Hornets!" I said. "Without Pom they would have an easier time beating us in the competition tomorrow."

"You're right," Ashley said. "They do have a strong motive." She chewed her pencil. "But we don't have any evidence against the Hornets."

"Not yet," I said. "But we might soon."

I unlocked the door of our equipment shed and turned on the light. Then Ashley and I searched all over the small window-less room.

"Nothing," I said. "No costume. No clues."

Ashley bent down and looked closely at the lock on the door.

"What are you doing?" I asked.

"Checking to see if the lock was broken or forced open," she said.

"Was it?" I asked.

"Nope," she said. "Which means only one thing. Whoever took the costume…"

"Had a key to our shed," I finished.

"Only two people on our squad have a shed key," Ashley said. "The squad leader and the captain."

"I don't think Fiona is a good suspect," I said. "She has no reason for taking Pom. But what about Brooke?"

Ashley took out her notebook. "I'm already writing her name down."

I peered over her shoulder as she wrote: SUSPECT #2—BROOKE BARTON. MOTIVE—THINKS MASCOT SHOULD HAVE SMALLER ROLE IN ROUTINE.

"You're right!" I said. "Brooke thinks mascots are silly. And this morning she wanted to change the routine. We have to question her right now!"

I closed and locked the shed door. Then Ashley and I ran back across the practice field to the gym. The field was really muddy. I almost slipped in the wet grass. I looked down—and almost stepped in a big clue!

"Ashley, look!" I pointed at a weird footprint on the ground. "Do you think it's Pom's footprint?"

Ashley studied the print. "Well, we don't have ostriches in California," she said, "so I think someone was outside last night wearing Pom's costume."

I looked around for more footprints. "I don't see any more prints...."

"Maybe the rain washed them away," Ashley said. "Let's keep looking."

She walked slowly in the direction of the gym. She studied the ground carefully before taking each step.

I could hear cheers coming from the gym. Boy, they sure were loud!

Ashley gasped. "Mary-Kate, look what I found!"

I whirled around.

Ashley was kneeling on the muddy ground. She held up a purple satin hair ribbon. The exact kind of hair ribbon Brooke wears every day!

4

IT ALL POINTS TO BROOKE

"**C**ase closed!" I cheered. "Brooke took the mascot costume!"

Ashley pulled a small plastic evidence bag from our detective backpack. She tucked the muddy purple ribbon into the bag.

"It sure looks that way," Ashley said. "Brooke has a motive. She had an opportunity to take the costume because she has a key to the shed. And we just found her hair ribbon in the field near Pom's footprint!"

"Let's go talk to her," I said, "and find out where Pom is."

We ran the rest of the way to the gym. Our squad was in the middle of a routine. They looked really good. The line was straight, and everyone's hand and body movements matched. I knew that if we found Pom in time, we would beat the Hornets for sure!

Kris spotted us. "Did you find Pom?"

"Not yet," Ashley said.

Everyone groaned.

"But we have an idea who took the costume," I said, staring hard at Brooke.

"Which one of the Hornets did it?" Princess Patty asked.

"I bet it was Tory Orsini," Kris muttered.

"Listen up, girls," Fiona said. "I'm sure Mary-Kate and Ashley will find Pom soon. But right now we have to practice our tumbling. So let's get down on the floor and stretch our muscles."

We all sat down on the shiny gym floor. Ashley and I plopped down on either side of Brooke.

"Hey, Brooke," I said. "We have something to show you."

Ashley took the purple hair ribbon out of the plastic bag and held it out to Brooke. "Is this yours?"

Brooke took the ribbon. "Hey, yeah! Where did you find it?"

"Out on the practice field," I said. "What was it doing out there?"

Brooke shrugged. "I guess it fell out of my hair at practice yesterday."

We all moved into a stretch. I could feel every muscle in my legs tighten.

"Were you outside last night?" I asked.

"No. Why?" Brooke said.

"We were out in the field just now, and we found Pom's footprint in the mud," Ashley said.

"And we found your purple ribbon near Pom's footprint," I continued. "*And* you're the only one on the squad with a key to the equipment shed."

Brooke stared at me. "*What are you saying?*"

"Did you take Pom?" I blurted out.

Brooke turned beet red. "*No!*" she said. "I would *never* ruin our squad's chances at winning."

"Where do you keep the shed key at night?" Ashley asked.

"On my dresser," Brooke said.

"Was it missing at all last night?" I asked.

Brooke shook her head.

Caitlin, who was sitting next to me, leaned over. "Well, my favorite extra-large towel is missing," she said.

"We'll try to help you find it," I told her.

"Attention, girls!" Fiona called. "Let's line up for tumbling passes."

Ashley pulled me aside. "Do you think Brooke is telling the truth?" she whispered.

I glanced at Brooke. "I don't know," I said. "I think we should keep her on the list."

"And the Hornets too," Ashley said, pointing across the gym.

Tory, the Hornets' bumblebee mascot, was in the middle of an amazing routine. All the Hornets clapped and cheered as Tory did an awesome somersault.

"We need to search their dorm for Pom," I said.

"Okay, girls," Fiona shouted. "Straighten out that line. Ready, and . . ."

"Eagles! Eagles! Mighty birds!
Victory! Victory! Hear our words!
Catch the fever! Hear our chants!
Watch us do our victory dance!"

We ran through the cheer a few more times, but we couldn't get it right. I think everyone's mind was on the missing mascot and not the cheer.

Fiona blew her whistle. "Your timing is completely off! Let's try it again."

This time we all performed our flying splits perfectly. Fiona clapped and hollered. "Good job, girls!"

Patty flopped onto the floor. "I'm all cheered out, Fiona. Don't you think it's time to relax? Maybe work on our tans?"

Fiona laughed. "Okay, break time. Have fun for the next two hours. We'll practice again after lunch."

Everyone headed to our dorm. Ashley and I had another plan. We were going to the Hornets' dorm to search for Pom.

Brooke walked down the path a few yards in front of us. "Where is Brooke going?" Ashley asked.

Our dorm sat on the right side of the grassy square. But Brooke took the path going to the left.

"Let's follow her," Ashley whispered.

I shook my head. "No," I said. "We need to check out the Hornets!"

"But Brooke is still one of our suspects," Ashley said.

She had a point. "Okay," I said.

We followed Brooke down the path.

I gasped. "Brooke is going into the Hornets' dorm!"

Ashley looked thoughtful. "Hmm...I wonder if we were wrong when we thought we had two different suspects," she said.

I understood what she meant. "Maybe Brooke is working with the Hornets." I said. "Maybe they took Pom *together*!"

5

SURPRISE IN THE CLOSET

We hid behind some bushes and watched Brooke enter the Hornets' dorm.

"We have to find out what she's doing in there," Ashley said.

"But how are we going to get in?"

I pointed to the front door. Two Hornet girls stood outside, drinking cans of soda and talking. We couldn't go in that way.

"I have an idea," Ashley said. "Come on!"

I followed her around to the side of the

building. Ashley pointed to a trellis—a wooden frame that looks like a ladder. If the Hornets' dorm was like ours, it led right up the wall of the building to a hall window on the second floor.

"You've got to be kidding!" I wailed. "We can't climb up there!"

"Why not? It's our only way in," Ashley said. "Come on, Mary-Kate, it's not that high. You said you wanted to get over your fear of heights today."

"But I was still getting used to the top of my dresser," I muttered.

We looked around to make sure no one was nearby. Then we ran to the trellis.

"You can go first, Mary-Kate," Ashley said.

"Gee, thanks!" I said.

"That's what sisters are for," she said with a smile. "Don't fall!"

I tested the trellis with one sneaker. It

seemed steady. I started to climb. About halfway up, the trellis creaked. I clutched the frame as tightly as I could. My knuckles turned white.

Don't look down, don't look down, I chanted to myself.

I started climbing again. *Left foot, right foot.* I felt the trellis move as Ashley started to climb. I stopped. My heart pounded. Would the trellis hold both of us?

I wanted to go back down, but I couldn't. Ashley was in my way. So I kept climbing.

Finally I reached the window and scrambled inside. I let out a huge breath.

I made it! And it was way higher than our pyramid!

"Great job, Mary-Kate," Ashley said as she slipped through the window.

"Thanks, Ashley," I said. "Now let's see what we can find out about Brooke and the Hornets."

We tiptoed down the hall and stopped right outside the living room. Carefully we peered around the door. There was Brooke—and Tory! They were giggling about something. Then Brooke reached out and gave Tory a hug!

Ashley grabbed my hand and pulled me away from the door. I followed her down the hallway.

"See?" I whispered. "I bet they took Pom together."

"Let's check out Tory's room," Ashley said.

We headed down the hall. Everyone's names were written on message boards that hung on the doors, just like in our dorm. Soon we found Tory's room.

I hesitated. We knew where Tory was, but what about her roommate? Was she in the room? There was only one way to find out. I bit my lip and knocked on the door.

No answer. Slowly I pushed the door open. Ashley and I peered in.

The room was empty. And messy!

"You take that side, and I'll check this side," Ashley said. "We don't have much time."

I dug through piles of dirty clothes on the bed and on the floor. No Pom.

I picked up the pile of pom-poms stashed in a corner. The yellow-and-black streamers had silver sparkles running through them.

"These are so cool!" I held one up to show Ashley.

Ashley looked up from the drawer she was searching. "Very cool."

I checked under the bed. Nothing.

I was trying to decide where else to look when I heard voices from down the hall. It sounded like Brooke and Tory. And they were coming toward us!

Ashley and I froze for a second. Then I ran to the window. There was no trellis and it was too high to jump! That left only under the bed or in the closet.

"Ashley, quick! The closet!" I whispered.

Ashley reached the closet first. She yanked open the door. It was packed tight with hanging clothes, but somehow she squeezed in.

I looked around wildly. I could hear Tory's voice just outside the room. I had only a second—and there was no room in the closet for me!

"Straddle shoulder sit!" Ashley whispered. "Now!"

A straddle shoulder sit is one of the cheerleading stunts we learned at camp this summer.

Ashley took a step out of the closet and bent her knees. I placed one of my sneakers on her thigh. Holding her shoulders, I

pushed myself up and swung my other leg around her head. I ended up sitting on Ashley's shoulders.

Ashley carefully backed into the closet. I pulled the door closed just as Brooke and Tory entered the room. *Whew!*

Sundresses and T-shirts covered my face. The clothing bar pressed against my back. I held my breath and tried to keep my body still.

"I can't believe you think it's a big deal," Tory was saying right outside the closet door. "It was just a joke. I'll give it back."

"Well, you'd better," Brooke said. "You should have asked me first."

Tory laughed. "Like you would have said it was okay to take it!"

She did it! She did it! I thought. *Tory took Pom!*

"Let's stop arguing about it for one second," Brooke said. "I need a favor. My big

white sweatshirt is missing. Can I borrow yours?"

"Sure," said Tory. "Just look in the closet."

The closet? Oh, no!

The door to the closet swung open—and there stood Brooke.

Her mouth fell open. She looked so surprised that I almost giggled.

Slowly I raised a finger to my lips.

My heart beat wildly.

What would Brooke do? Would she tell Tory we were here?

6

DID TORY TAKE POM?

Brooke slammed the door right in our faces.

I smiled in the darkness. I could feel Ashley let out her breath.

"Actually, it's kind of warm for a sweatshirt," Brooke said to Tory. "Want to go down to the vending machine in the basement for a soda? I've got lots of change."

"A free soda?" Tory asked. "Yes!"

"And I'm taking back my teddy bear! I

can't believe you stole him from my room and dressed him in Hornet colors!" Brooke said.

"I said it was a joke," Tory said.

I could hear them walk out of the room. Brooke closed the door loudly.

Ashley wasted no time opening the closet door. We both tumbled out.

"That was our closest call ever," I said.

"Too close," Ashley agreed. "Let's get out of here!"

We ran down the hall and tiptoed down the stairs. There weren't any Hornets in sight. We sneaked out the front door of the Hornets' dorm and rushed across the square to our own dorm.

When we reached our room, I flopped down on my bed, trying to catch my breath. Ashley flopped onto hers.

"Do you think Tory took Pom?" I asked Ashley. "She definitely took something that

didn't belong to her. That's what Brooke said."

Before Ashley could answer there was a knock on our door.

"Come in," I called. I sat up.

Brooke walked in. She sat next to me on my bed and started to laugh.

"What were you guys doing in Tory's room?" she asked. "You freaked me out when I opened the closet!"

"We were snooping," Ashley said. "What were *you* doing with Tory?"

"Tory is my cousin," Brooke said.

"Really?" I asked. "How come you never told us that?"

"I didn't want anyone to know that my cousin is a Hornet," Brooke said. "I still totally want to beat her in the *Cheer Off!*"

"So you didn't help the Hornets take Pom?" I asked.

"No way!" Brooke exclaimed. "I told you

that before. I had nothing to do with Pom's disappearance. That's why I went to see Tory."

"What do you mean?" Ashley asked.

"I thought maybe Tory would tell me if the Hornets took Pom," Brooke said.

"Did she?" I asked.

Brooke shook her head. "No."

"Then what were you and Tory talking about? You said she took something," Ashley said.

Brooke laughed. She held out a small stuffed animal. "She took my teddy bear and dressed it in yellow and black as a joke."

She got off my bed and headed for the door. "I'm going to eat lunch. You guys coming?"

"In a minute," Ashley said. "We'll meet you there."

Brooke waved and shut the door.

Ashley pulled out her detective note-book. "I think we should cross Brooke off our list," she said.

"You're right," I said. "I believe her story. If she wasn't telling the truth, she would have let Tory know we were hiding in her closet. But that only leaves the Hornets."

Ashley put a line through Brooke's name.

"Let's see if we can find out more about the Hornets at lunch," Ashley said.

She went to her dresser and started to brush out her hair. "Hey, can I borrow your purple sparkle nail polish? It will match our uniforms."

"Sure, Ashley." I went to my dresser to get it. But the nail polish wasn't where I kept it.

"That's funny," I said. "My purple nail polish is missing."

Ashley put down her brush and turned to

me. "Something *else* is missing? That is so—"

"Whoever did this is in *soooo* much trouble!" someone shrieked.

"That sounds like Patty!" I said.

Ashley and I went to our door and looked out. So did Caitlin and Briana, who lived across the hall.

The first thing we saw were feathers. Hundreds and hundreds of white feathers floated down the hall in our direction. And in the middle of the storm of feathers stood Patty!

Had Patty found Pom?

7

BIRDS OF A FEATHER

Patty stomped up to our door and shook two feather pillows in front of us. The tops of the pillows were cut open, and feathers spilled out everywhere.

"Somebody destroyed my pillows!" Patty shrieked. "Look! Half the feathers are missing! Missing!"

"Calm down, Patty," Ashley said. "They're only pillows."

"Only pillows?" Patty cried. "My parents

bought these pillows in Europe. They are the only ones I can sleep on. Who would do such a horrible thing?"

"I don't know, Patty," I said.

Patty's face turned fire-engine red. "Well, you two are detectives. It's your job to figure out mysteries. I'm hiring you to figure out this one—now!"

I felt terrible for Patty. She was almost in tears.

I turned to Ashley. "I think we have two mysteries to solve."

Ashley knit her brows together. "There's a lot of stuff missing around here," she said slowly.

"You're right, Ashley," I said. "And it all started this morning when Pom disappeared!"

"What else is missing?" Briana asked.

Ashley started to list the missing things. "My hair dryer and Caitlin's towel. Brooke

said her sweatshirt is missing. Mary-Kate couldn't find her purple nail polish. And now Patty's pillows are missing their feathers...."

"That's a strange list," I said. "Why would anyone want to take those things?"

"I don't care why," Patty snapped. "I just want my feathers back!"

"We need to get Pom back too," Caitlin said.

Ashley gasped. "I think I know who took Pom!"

8

ANOTHER SUSPECT

"**W**ho?" Patty, Caitlin, Briana, and I cried together. "Who took Pom?"

Ashley flipped open her detective notebook and scribbled something down. I tried to read over her shoulder, but she was writing too fast.

"Ashley, tell me!" I said.

"The person who took Pom," Ashley said, "is the same person who took all the other missing things. We don't have two

mysteries to solve. We only have one big mystery!"

"What do you mean?" I asked.

Ashley showed me her notebook.

I read the list of missing things out loud: "My hair dryer, Caitlin's towel, Brooke's big white sweatshirt, Mary-Kate's purple nail polish, and Patty's pillow feathers.

"I get it!" I jumped up and down. "Most of those things have to do with the Pom costume! Pom has feathers and wears a big white sweatshirt. And the sweatshirt has a purple #1 written on it!"

Briana scratched her head. "But how are the mysteries connected?"

"I'm not totally sure yet," Ashley admitted. "But I bet whoever has all our missing things has Pom too. So this gives us more to investigate."

I nodded. "It will make it easier to find out who did it."

"It better," Patty said, her hands on her hips. "I need my pillows restuffed before bedtime! Or else!"

After lunch our squad got together on the field for afternoon practice. The sun had dried up most of the mud.

We ran five laps around the field before we did our stretches. Fiona made warm-ups fun by playing the radio. We did our sit-ups and push-ups to the sound of the beat.

When warm-ups were finished, Fiona called us over. "How are you guys doing on the case?"

"We're getting closer," I said. "But we haven't found Pom yet."

Fiona looked serious. She sighed. "Okay, girls. We should come up with another routine, just in case we don't find Pom in time."

She blew her whistle to call the other

girls over. "We need to get a new mascot costume and come up with a new routine. *And* practice the pyramid. We haven't practiced the pyramid once all the way through yet."

"I think we should wait until later," Kris said. "I'll go call some costume stores now and see if I can find a costume like Pom."

"Can't that wait until later?" Emma asked.

"No, it can't," Kris said. "I need to practice the double back handspring with the costume on. It's harder to do with the costume."

Before Fiona could say anything, Kris took off. She headed toward the main building.

I thought I would be relieved, but I felt more nervous than ever.

"Do you know that I've never jumped off the top of the pyramid?" I said to Ashley. "Not once. How will I be able to do it in the

Cheer Off! if Kris is never around when it's time to practice the pyramid?"

Ashley grabbed my arm. "What did you say about Kris?"

"Kris is never around to do the double back handspring at the end of the pyramid stunt," I said. "She always has an excuse. Her costume is missing, or—"

"Mary-Kate, have you ever seen Kris do a double back handspring?" Ashley asked.

"Well...yeah, at the beginning of the week. Kris and Emma both did it. But I've never seen Kris do it with the Pom costume on."

"And she keeps saying how heavy the costume is. She says cheering is harder with the costume on," Ashley pointed out. "I bet it's tricky to do the double back handspring with the bird costume on."

Suddenly I understood. "Kris is scared, like I am," I said. "She's scared about doing

the stunt at the end of the pyramid. That's why she keeps running away every time she's supposed to do it!"

"If Kris is having trouble with the double back handspring," Ashley said slowly, "then maybe she hid Pom."

"Yes! Kris has a motive for getting rid of the Pom costume," I said. "Without the costume, we have to change the routine!"

Ashley took out her detective notebook. "Mary-Kate, we have another suspect!"

9

TIME IS RUNNING OUT

Ashley and I dashed to the main building. The only phone we campers were allowed to use was in the office. Kris stood near the desk flipping through the yellow pages of a large phone book.

"What's up, guys?" Kris asked when she spotted us.

"We need to talk to you," I said. "It's important."

Kris shrugged. "Okay." She followed us

across the hall to the lounge. We all sat on one of the cushy brown sofas.

I decided to get right to the point. We were running out of time. "Kris, were you the one who took Pom?"

Kris's blue eyes widened. "Me?" she asked. "Why would you think that?"

"Whenever it's time to practice the pyramid, you disappear. And we've never seen you do the double back handspring with the Pom costume on. So we thought you might have hidden Pom so you wouldn't have to do it," I said.

Kris chewed on one of her fingernails.

Ashley and I waited. *Was Kris about to confess?*

"I did it," Kris said. She stood up and paced around the room. "I was—I am—scared. I don't think I can do the double back handspring with the Pom costume on. I don't want our squad to lose because of

me. I thought getting rid of Pom was the answer...."

I didn't say anything. I could almost understand why she did it.

Kris sat down. "But I only hid Pom once—that time in the laundry room. Really! I didn't take the costume this time!"

I grabbed Ashley. "We'll be right back, Kris." We walked back across the hall to the office.

"Do you believe her, Mary-Kate?" Ashley asked.

"I think she's telling the truth," I said. "Kris was looking up costume stores in the phone book. If she knows where Pom is why would she do that?"

Ashley pulled out her detective notebook. She crossed Kris off our suspect list. We walked back over to her.

"We believe you," I said to Kris.

Kris let out a breath. "Whew! I was

afraid you wouldn't." She stood up. "I'd better go. I need to find another costume!"

Kris left.

Ashley tapped her pencil against the opened page of her notebook. "Now what?" she asked me. "We keep crossing suspects off our list."

"What about what you were saying before lunch? About the missing things being connected?" I pointed to the list in her notebook. "Let's go over that again."

"Okay." Ashley read the list out loud. "My hair dryer. Caitlin's towel. Brooke's sweatshirt. Your nail polish. And Patty's pillow feathers."

"Well, that leaves only Kris, Emma, and Briana who didn't have anything taken," I said. "We know Kris is innocent. So I guess we should check out Emma and Briana."

Ashley jumped up. "Let's go peek around their rooms."

The sun was high in the sky as we walked past our equipment shed to our dorm.

"Hey, what's that twinkling over there?" Ashley asked.

She pointed to something shiny gleaming in the grass by the side of the shed. We ran over to check it out.

"We must have missed something this morning when it was so gray out," I said.

Ashley reached down and picked it up. It was a silver charm.

A silver megaphone charm.

Emma's charm!

10

SMILE FOR THE CAMERA

"**E**mma didn't have any of her stuff taken. And here's her charm, by the shed where Pom's costume was stolen." I was thinking out loud. "We have a new suspect, Ashley!"

Ashley rolled the silver charm around in her hand. She wrinkled up her eyebrows. She always does that when she's thinking especially hard.

"But why Emma?" she asked finally.

"What could be her motive for taking Pom?"

Good question.

"I don't know," I admitted. "Let's go talk to her." We headed back to the practice field.

I pulled Emma aside.

"Emma, look what we just found." I pointed to the charm in Ashley's hand. "When did you lose it?"

"Wow!" Emma exclaimed. "You found it! Great! It's my lucky charm. I lost it yesterday afternoon when Patty and I went to the shed to get the pom-poms. Thanks!" She took the charm from Ashley.

Ashley and I walked to the side of the field.

"We keep thinking we have a suspect, and then we keep hitting dead ends," I said.

"We still have the Hornets on the list," Ashley reminded me.

I sighed. "I'm beginning to think we're never going to solve this case."

Ashley patted me on the shoulder. "The Trenchcoat Twins never give up!"

Across the field, I watched Fiona reach into her nylon duffel bag. "Anyone want to see the squad photo?" she called.

We all gathered around.

"Hey, Brooke!" Ashley said. "Your pom-pom is covering half my face!"

"Sorry!" Brooke giggled. "At least you're smiling. I look like I swallowed a fly!"

"I should have worn shinier lip gloss," Patty complained.

I giggled. Princess Patty's lips were so shiny in the picture I didn't see how they could be any shinier. That's when I saw it.

"Can I take a closer look at the picture?" I asked Fiona.

"Sure," she said, handing it to me.

I looked at the photo again carefully. *Yes!*

I pulled Ashley aside.

"What do you see?" Ashley asked.

"Look closely at Emma," I said.

Ashley gasped. "Emma is wearing her silver megaphone charm!"

"Right," I said. "And this squad photo was taken *after* she got the pom-poms out of the shed yesterday afternoon."

"That means one thing," Ashley said. "Emma lied to us!"

11

FOLLOW THAT FEATHER

"**W**e need to talk to Emma again!" Ashley exclaimed.

I glanced at our squad. Emma was gone.

"Where did Emma go?" I asked.

No one had seen her slip away.

"Let's check her room!" Ashley said.

We jogged across the field to our dorm. We burst through the door and ran up the stairs two at a time. We raced down the hall. I pushed open the door to the room

that Emma shared with Brooke. No one was there.

Ashley flicked on the light. "Let's do a quick search for evidence," she said.

I found a pair of muddy sneakers in the closet. "Look, Ashley!"

Ashley shook her head. "Muddy sneakers could mean anything," she said.

"But this could only mean one thing," I said, holding up a white feather.

"Evidence!" Ashley cried.

She slipped the feather into an evidence bag and we hurried out of the dorm.

We paused in the grassy square. *Where did Emma go?* I wondered.

Whirr whirr.

"Ashley, do you hear that?"

Whirr whirr.

"Yes!" Ashley cried. "It sounds like my super-powerful hair dryer!"

"The noise is coming from right here!" I

pointed to the building we were standing next to.

Fiona told us that most of her classes took place in this building. Since it was summer, the building was closed. At least, it was supposed to be closed....

"Let's check it out!" Ashley said.

We followed the sound of the hair dryer down to the last classroom at the end of the hall.

Ashley and I burst through the door.

Emma's head snapped up. She looked surprised to see us. And we were surprised too! Because Emma was sitting on the floor, blow-drying Pom the Wonder Bird!

Emma turned off the dryer. "I didn't think you two would figure it out so fast," she said.

Ashley and I sat down beside her on the floor. I coughed. White feathers floated everywhere. Caitlin's towel, Brooke's

sweatshirt, and my purple nail polish sat on a nearby desk.

"Emma," Ashley said. "I can't believe it was you. Why did you take Pom? I thought you wanted our squad to beat the Hornets."

"I do!" Emma said. "That's why I took Pom."

"I don't understand," I said.

"I knew Kris was afraid to do her double back handspring in the mascot costume." Emma fluffed Pom's feathers as she spoke. "I wanted to show everyone that I could do the stunt in the Pom costume. Then Kris would have to let me be the mascot!"

"So you took the costume last night?" I asked.

Emma nodded. "When everyone was asleep I took the key to the shed off Brooke's dresser. I put on the costume and went out to the field to practice. I knew it would be hard to do the double back hand-

spring in the heavy bird outfit. I wanted to make sure I could really do it."

"And then the thunderstorm started," Ashley guessed.

"The rain poured down out of nowhere!" Emma said. "I got soaked. I tried to run, but the feathers really weighed me down. I tripped and fell right into the mud. Pom got all wet and muddy, and its sweatshirt ripped."

"That's why you took everyone's stuff," I said. "To fix Pom, right?"

"Right," said Emma. "I didn't want to get into trouble for taking Pom. I thought I could dry Pom today and slip it back into the shed. I always planned for Pom to be back for tomorrow's finals."

I pointed to my purple sparkle nail polish. "I get why you needed the other stuff. What's my nail polish for?"

"To paint the #1 on the sweatshirt."

Emma sighed and looked around the room. "It's much harder to fix Pom than I thought."

She hung her head. "I guess I ruined our chance to beat the Hornets. I'm really sorry."

Ashley stood up. "I have an idea. Wait here." She hurried out of the room.

A few minutes later the entire Eagles squad trooped through the doorway. I could tell Ashley had filled everyone in.

"We're all going to work together to fix Pom," she announced.

Ashley, Emma, and Briana tackled blow-drying Pom. Brooke and I painted the sweatshirt. Kris cleaned the mud off the rest of the bird. And, believe it or not, Princess Patty glued her pillow feathers onto Pom's bare patches!

As we worked, Caitlin cheered:

"Thank you, Ashley!
Thank you, Mary-Kate!

Because of you, we're gonna be great!
Go team!"

I jumped as high as I could and let out a whoop. We just finished the second-to-last cheer of our routine. We were awesome. One more routine and I knew we would be the winners of *Cheer Off!*

I could see Tory and the other Hornets watching from the sidelines. Brooke gave the signal. It was time for the pyramid.

My heart began to speed up—not from fear but from excitement.

The bases moved into position. Then the two spotters helped Emma and Ashley up.

It was my turn. As I climbed, our squad chanted:

"We're going to the top,
Going straight to the top,
Going up, going up, going up!"

When I reached the top of the pyramid, I raised my arms high. I looked down. Where was Kris?

Then I saw her—she was dressed as Pom the Wonder Bird. Fast as lightning, Kris ran across the field…and flew into the most awesome double back handspring.

Nobody moved, but I knew our entire squad was cheering—on the inside!

Kris placed the inflatable nest underneath the pyramid.

"You can do it," Ashley whispered from below me.

I smiled…and jumped. The next second I landed right in the middle of the inflatable nest.

I did it!

Our squad gathered around me, screaming and jumping and hollering.

A few minutes later, the announcer's voice boomed over the loudspeaker.

"Congratulate the winners of this year's *Cheer Off!*—the Eagles!"

We all jumped up and down and hugged each other. Fiona was so happy she cried. And Caitlin made up one more chant:

"Eagles! Eagles! It's time to celebrate!
Thanks to Ashley and to Mary-Kate!"

Hi from both of us,

Have you heard the legend of the tattooed cat? The tattooed cat is a black cat with a white mark in the shape of a jack-o'-lantern. If you pet it before midnight on Halloween and make a wish, your wish will come true. I wanted to find the tattooed cat, but Ashley said there is no such thing as a lucky cat.

That's when we saw a sign with a picture of the tattooed cat! The cat was lost! Want to find out what happened? Check out the next page for a sneak peek at *The New Adventures of Mary-Kate & Ashley: The Case Of The Tattooed Cat.*

See you next time!

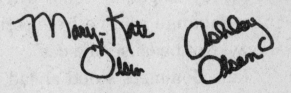

A sneak peek at our next mystery…

The Case Of The
TATTOOED CAT

"I *really* want to find the tattooed cat this year," I said. "And Halloween is the day after tomorrow—so time is running out!"

"Oh, come on, Mary-Kate." My sister Ashley gave my shoulder a little push. "You don't believe the tattooed cat is real, do you?"

"Yes, I do," I said. "And if I find it—I mean *when* I find it—I'll win the spelling bee for sure."

Ashley laughed. "You'll win the spelling bee because you've been studying like crazy! Not because of a cat."

Jane Sommers stood ahead of us at the

candy counter in Chessa's Candies, our favorite candy store. She turned to face us. "What are you guys talking about?" she asked.

"You've never heard of the tattooed cat?" our friend, Tim Park asked. He looked amazed.

Jane shook her head.

"It's a lucky cat," I said. "If you see the cat on Halloween and pet it three times before the clock strikes midnight, you can make a wish. And your wish will come true!"

"Wow!" Jane said. "What does the cat look like?"

"It's black," Tim said, "and it's got a white tattoo on its neck in the shape of a jack-o'-lantern."

Jane's eyebrows shot up. "A lucky cat! And it has a real tattoo?"

"Yes," I said. "That's what's supposed to make it lucky."

Ashley shook her head. "There is no such thing as a lucky cat."

"There is so!" Tim said. "I can prove it."

"Really?" I said. This time my eyebrows shot up! "Have you seen the cat?"

"No, but..." Tim glanced around the candy store. There were lots of kids from school in the store.

He lowered his voice. We all gathered around him. "I heard a kid who goes to Washington Elementary School found the cat last year. My cousin Billy told me."

"That's not proof," Ashley said.

"Ashley is right." I sighed. "But that doesn't mean the cat *doesn't* exist either!"

This time Ashley sighed. Then she looked at her pink plastic watch. "Come on, Mary-Kate. We have to get home."

"Good-bye, guys! See you tomorrow!" I grabbed my backpack and followed my sister out of the store.

I turned to Ashley. "If we see the tattooed

cat when we go trick-or-treating, what will you wish for?"

Ashley shrugged. "I haven't thought about it," she said, "because there is no such thing."

Ashley is always so logical. Sometimes it's fun not to be so logical.

We headed down the sidewalk. That's when I saw it. I grabbed Ashley's arm. "Look! Do you see what I see?"

Taped to a telephone pole, right in front of us, was a handmade sign. I read the sign out loud: "Missing cat."

I stared at the picture. It was a picture of a black cat. A black cat with a white jack-o'-lantern tattoo!

"It's the tattooed cat!" I yelled.

THE NEW ADVENTURES OF MARY-KATE & ASHLEY™
Camp Survival Kit Sweepstakes

OFFICIAL RULES:

1. No purchase necessary.

2. To enter complete the official entry form or hand print your name, address, age, and phone number along with the words "THE NEW ADVENTURES OF MARY-KATE & ASHLEY Camp Survival Kit Sweepstakes" on a 3" x 5" card and mail to THE NEW ADVENTURES OF MARY-KATE & ASHLEY Camp Survival Kit Sweepstakes, c/o HarperEntertainment, Attn: Children's Marketing Department, 10 East 53rd Street, New York, NY 10022. Entries must be received no later than October 31, 2003. Enter as often as you wish, but each entry must be mailed separately. One entry per envelope. Partially completed, illegible, or mechanically reproduced entries will not be accepted. Sponsors are not responsible for lost, late, mutilated, illegible, stolen, postage due, incomplete, or misdirected entries. All entries become the property of Dualstar Entertainment Group, LLC, and will not be returned.

3. Sweepstakes open to all legal residents of the United States (excluding Colorado and Rhode Island), who are between the ages of five and fifteen on October 31, 2003, excluding employees and immediate family members of HarperCollins Publishers, Inc ("HarperCollins"), Parachute Properties and Parachute Press, Inc., and their respective subsidiaries and affiliates, officers, directors, shareholders, employees, agents, attorneys, and other representatives (individually and collectively "Parachute"), Dualstar Entertainment Group, LLC, and its subsidiaries and affiliates, officers, directors, shareholders, employees, agents, attorneys, and other representatives (individually and collectively "Dualstar"), and their respective parent companies, affiliates, subsidiaries, advertising, promotion and fulfillment agencies, and the persons with whom each of the above are domiciled. Offer void where prohibited or restricted by law.

4. Odds of winning depend on the total number of entries received. Approximately 400,000 sweepstakes announcements published. All prizes will be awarded. Winners will be randomly drawn on or about November 15, 2003, by HarperCollins, whose decisions are final. Potential winner will be notified by mail and will be required to sign and return an affidavit of eligibility and release of liability within 14 days of notification. Prizes won by minors will be awarded to parent or legal guardian who must sign and return all required legal documents. By acceptance of the prize, winner consents to the use of his or her name, photograph, likeness and biographical information by HarperCollins, Parachute, Dualstar, and for publicity purposes without further compensation except where prohibited.

5. One (1) Grand Prize Winner wins a Camp Survival Kit to include the following items: a backpack, personal CD player, sunglasses, photo frame and three music CDs from the *mary-kateandashley* brand; a hat, stationery, a journal, three pens, 20 first-class postage stamps, an address book; one autographed copy of each of the following books from THE NEW ADVENTURES OF MARY-KATE & ASHLEY book series: THE CASE OF THE SUMMER CAMP CAPER, THE CASE OF THE CHEERLEADING CAMP MYSTERY, THE CASE OF THE DOG CAMP MYSTERY, and THE CASE OF CAMP CROOKED LAKE. Approximate retail value: $210.00.

6. Only one prize will be awarded per individual, family, or household. Prizes are non-transferable and cannot be substituted, sold or redeemed for cash. Any federal, state, or local taxes are the responsibility of the winner. Sponsor may substitute prize of equal or greater retail value, if necessary, at its sole discretion.

7. Additional terms: By participating, entrants agree a) to the official rules and decisions of the judges, which will be final in all respects, and to waive any claim to ambiguity of the official rules and b) to release, discharge, and hold harmless HarperCollins, Parachute, Dualstar, and their affiliates, subsidiaries, and advertising and promotion agencies from and against any and all liability or damages associated with acceptance, use, or misuse of any prize received in this sweepstakes.

8. Any dispute arising from this Sweepstakes will be determined according to the laws of the State of New York, without reference to its conflict of law principles, and the entrants consent to the personal jurisdiction of the State and Federal courts located in New York County and agree that such courts have exclusive jurisdiction over all such disputes.

9. To obtain the name of the winners, please send your request and a self-addressed stamped envelope (residents of Vermont may omit return postage) to THE NEW ADVENTURES OF MARY-KATE & ASHLEY Camp Survival Kit Sweepstakes Winners, c/o HarperEntertainment, Attn: Children's Marketing Department, 10 East 53rd Street, New York, NY 10022 by December 1, 2003. Sweepstakes Sponsor: HarperCollins Publishers, Inc.

MARY-KATE AND ASHLEY in ACTION!

BOOK SERIES

Based on the hit animated television series

Special Agents Misty and Amber are off to save the world . . . again! With cool high-tech gear, a private jet, and their friends by their side, Mary-Kate and Ashley go undercover to track down super villians and stop their evil plans!

№ SEVEN

based on the hit tv series

MARY-KATE AND ASHLEY in ACTION!

Episode 7: PASSWORD: RED HOT

Let's go save the world... again!

Win Mary-Kate and Ashley in ACTION! doll

Don't miss the other books in the

MARY-KATE AND ASHLEY in ACTION! book series!

Coming soon wherever books are sold!

- ❏ Makeup Shake-Up
- ❏ The Dream Team
- ❏ Fubble Bubble Trouble
- ❏ Operation Evaporation
- ❏ Dog-Gone Mess
- ❏ The Music Meltdown

Real Books for Real Girls™

HarperEntertainment
An Imprint of HarperCollinsPublishers
www.harpercollins.com

PARACHUTE PRESS

DUALSTAR PUBLICATIONS

AMERICA Online

mary-kateandashley.com
America Online Keyword: mary-kateandashley

MEET CAITLIN!

Her parents know she is a BIG Mary-Kate and Ashley fan, so they bid for and won the chance for her to "Be a Character in a Mary-Kate and Ashley book" during a recent auction held to help raise money for Multiple Sclerosis research.

Born Caitlin Marie, she is often called Katie by her close friends. Katie has watched all of the Mary-Kate and Ashley movies, watches their television series, *Two of a Kind* and *So Little Time*, and reads their books. Her favorite books are those in the *Two of a Kind* series and *Two of a Kind Diaries*.

When she's not watching or reading Mary-Kate and Ashley works, Katie spends time with her family and friends, plays soccer, plays basketball, goes to movies, shops at the mall and swims in her pool. She is also in Girl Scouts. Katie's favorite vacation spots are Disneyland and Orlando, FL. Katie also likes visiting relatives in Arizona.

Katie's family thinks she's a "crack-up" because she is always making them laugh. Her favorite foods are salads and fruits, and for dessert, chocolate. Katie tries hard in school. Her favorite subjects are writing, spelling and recess.

Katie feels lucky to be included in a Mary-Kate and Ashley book.

Coming soon...A new
mary-kateandashley
2004 calendar!

 DUALSTAR CONSUMER PRODUCTS

mead.

Look for the latest in  posters